My Mafioso Stepbrother

My brother, well stepbrother is Tommy Sicardo. He is the head of the Chicago south-suburbs'/northwest Indiana family, Ted that one. The mafia. Since we are basically right next to

Chicago, the majority of the drugs and guns going in or out of the city goes through Tommy. Tommy is the youngest local boss that the Italian American mafia has ever had. You see mama was daddy's second wife. Daddy's first wife died, I'm not exactly sure how but it happened when Tommy was young. And my mom had me really young, my bio dad was never in the picture so when my mom and Tommy's dad got married, I finally had a daddy and an older brother. Sadly, mom and dad were both gunned down 3 years ago in a organized crime war and at the time, even though Tommy was young, he was already working as

I

Daddy's right hand man and from what I have heard, already had a take no prisoners or kill or be killed mentality that Daddy drove into his head from the day he was born so he was a very efficient enforcer. Our Uncle Angelo, daddy's brother, is the head of the Chicago Chapter so I guess with Chicago being right next door to Northwest Indiana it was a no-brainer to place Tommy here so he could get his feet wet of being a made man while under the watchful eye of Uncle Angelo. Unfortunately for me though, within days of my parent's funeral, I was shipped off to boarding school the first chance Tommy had since

I was still a teenager when our parents died. But that all is about to change. I haven't really seen my stepbrother much since our parents died. Even on breaks or holidays, he either made me stay at the boarding school or paid for some lavish vacation like Europe or somewhere else to ship me off to during the whole break. I guess he couldn't be bothered to raise me or even see me after all. But now I got into trouble, big trouble. I'm only a week shy of turning 18 years old and only had a month to graduate boarding school but as of yesterday, I got kicked out of school. They have a "zero policy" for drinking and drugs, although I've ever only smoked pot and drank. I didn't get to talk to my brother when they called but was sitting in the chair at the Dean's office and I could hear Tommy yelling and cussing through the phone, something about I pay your school more than fucking enough to turn a blind eye one fucking time! And to my dismay, that's when the Dean informed my brother that this is not only my fourth time being caught but the last two times, I was the one who provided the alcohol and the pot to the other students. The Dean said at that point, Tommy just slammed the phone down and hung up on him. So, I'm on the plane about to land in a small airport in Gary Indiana, not to far from our home in Hammond Indiana. Over the decades, Hammond has had a increase in Gangs and crimes. But it is still home. Way back when, Mom and Dad had bought several homes and acres that backed up to the woods when they had first gotten married and knocked all the homes down and built one lavish mansion with a security entrance and a security fence brimming the whole property. Growing up, it sometimes felt that we lived in the country with the quiet and privacy we had. Over the years, more roads

and buildings have been
built surrounding our
family's property but it's
still quiet for the most
part.
I'm nervous, I don't know
why. It's not like I expect
my brother to pick me up.
God Forbid he made any
time for me but I am
actually nervous about
my Uncle being there.
Who knows if he had the

time to make it from Chicago but I hope not. The few minor issues I've had at school like low grades, I've dealt with my Uncle, not Tommy. Uncle Angelo always told Daddy when we were younger that he was to easy on us kids and spoiled us to much. So, Uncle Angelo would call me at school and yell and threaten to

your spine.
But I'm almost 18 now and Tommy is only eight years older and clearly doesn't live on the straight and narrow so I should have nothing to worry about with him. Tommy has never hurt me or scared me and if anything, he's too busy to be bothered with me.

Chapter 2

I descend down the stairs off of the plane at the small airport in Gary, Indiana. Right away, I see a sleek black Mercedes SUV with tinted windows waiting at the bottom for me. Great, it screams my brothers taste, my brother's car. On the positive, it isn't Uncle Angelo. I'm actually

excited to see Tommy, it
has been so long.

As soon as I reach the last
step, Tommy throws
open his driver side door
and steps out, taking fast
long strides near me.
Wow, did he grow up.
He's absolutely gorgeous!
He's tall, yet lean and
muscular. He is the
walking, talking saying
"tall, dark and handsome

" And my stepbrother! Geez! He's your brother Katie! I silently scold myself. He grabs my bag from the pilot, and I face him smiling about to say hello when Tommy grabs my arm forcefully, his fingers digging in to my upper arm and starts pulling me to the passenger side of his car. "Ow Tommy that hurts!

Stop it! I cry out!" I try to yank my arm away but his grip only tightens, making me Yelp in pain. He throws open the passenger door, roughly letting go of my arm "Get the fuck in the car!" he commands me. It hasn't gone unnoticed that he didn't even say hello.
I half stumble, half get

into the car and glare at him, not believing his nerve. I would expect this shit out of my Uncle Angelo but not my brother.

"Hello to you too" I say sarcastically looking at him and then purposely rolling my eyes.

"Not another fucking word till we get home Kathleen! NOT ONE

FUCKING WORD!"
Tommy roars. I jump as
he slams his own door
shut, peeling out of the
small ass airport. Wow,
he used my full name.
Everyone including him
always call me Katie. Only
Daddy and once or twice
Uncle Angelo would use
my full name when I did
something really bad as a
child or while at boarding

school, but never Tommy. As much as I hate to admit it, Tommy is hot as hell even when he's pissed and he is pissed! I just wish he wasn't pissed at me. I've never seen him like this. I don't know what to expect. I thought I was afraid of my uncle, and my brother was no big deal. I think I should have been worrying and

maybe even fearing
Tommy this whole time
too.

The house looks the same
when we pull up except
the number of guards
standing ready to open
our doors and guard the
property. It's more
guards and workers than
Daddy ever had. I try to
open my door and its
locked, controlled by the

master controls on the car which of course is controlled by Tommy. I turn back to look at him and he gives me a look that sends a chill down my spine. I get the hint, keep my mouth shut. And I wonder when he started giving "the look". He finally hits the unlock button and as the guards open our doors, I get out and follow Tommy in silence as we enter the house. He has made many renovations since I've been gone. Everything is updated, sleek and modern, it barely looks like the same house from the inside. The layout of the house is the same but that's about it. I'm surprised to find that my step-brother has actually really good taste in decorating. As I step in the house, I notice there are several people in the house working. Our family cook, Nora is getting dinner ready in the kitchen, as a maid tidy up and then a few more guards or goons either hanging out in the great room or they are waiting to do business with Tommy.

"Go to your room, I'll fucking deal with your dumb ass later." Tommy says as he starts striding to the office across from the great room. Oh, hell no! He did not just call me out like that in a room full of people! How dare he?! He is not going to embarrass me and send me to my room like I'm some troublesome small child! A child he clearly doesn't want here as he hasn't said anything to me except to curse me out and try to send me to my room! My God, I'm almost 18!

"Excuse me?" I call him out

He stops mid stride and turns on his heel and before I know it, he's

I

staring down at me, practically on top of me, his eyes full of anger, no not anger, Rage. His eyes are full of rage and what looks like hate.

"Do I really need to fucking repeat myself Katherine?" He Asks as he purposely draws out my full name again. The look in his eyes says it all. He is pissed, probably beyond pissed. But there is no way that I'm going to let him walk all over me, to bully me. He hasn't moved a inch waiting with a scowl on his face for my response.

"You clearly don't want me here and that's fine. I'll more than happily leave but don't think that you get to talk to me like that Tommy! Like I'm a child. I'm almost 18! I state

I didn't notice that as I was talking, I had been slowly backing up and now I have my back up against the far wall and Tommy had been keeping in step with me getting closer and closer until his face was even closer to my face and now I can't back up any further. I'm stuck.

"Don't talk to you as a child? " he asks incredulously, a wicked smile plays on his lips for a mere second before the rage comes back full force in the way he looks at me with complete disgust and the tone of his voice. "A child fucks around at school! A child plays stupid games and gets kicked out of boarding school! I paid DAMN good money for you to go there and then imagine my surprise when I'm told that this was your 4th or 5th infraction? Drinking? Smoking pot and doing God knows what else, corrupting the other kids that are at school for an education! What the

fucking hell is wrong with you? " he yells in my face "Your ass is grounded! Now go to your room!" He roars
I swallow, acutely aware that everyone in the house has fallen silent and is watching. He is NOT going to embarrass me like this in my own home! In our parents' home!

I

"Because gang-banging and drug dealing is so un-childlike right Mr. Mafia?" I asked as I temporarily forgotten my fear and exploded back at Tommy with a matched rage in my voice.

Chapter 3

SMACK
The side of my face is on

fire as I go flying sideways and hit the ground hard. That fucker hit me! He hit me! I'm disoriented for a few seconds. But before I could even process totally what had just happened, Tommy grabbed me by the front of my shirt and yanked me back up to a standing position, holding me up against the wall, my tip-toes barely touching the ground as he dangles me there, like a rag doll.

"Anything else?" He asked smirking as he holds me there without even trying. I'm no match for him. I see that but I am pissed and for the first time in my life, I'm scared of Tommy and royally embarrassed but I

don't want him to know
so i stupidly continue this
charade.

"FUCK YOU!" I spat in his
face
He raises his hand back
again and before I have
time to flinch much less
say anything,
SMACK
As he backhanded me, he
also let go of his hold on

me and i flew to the ground once more hitting even harder. I land face down on the floor, barely able to get my hands down fast enough to save my face from hitting the ceramic tile. Tears sting my eyes but I won't give him the satisfaction. I try to will the tears away. The fucker hit me again! And this time he got my lip. Its cracked and I feel it bleeding...

"We can keep doing this all-night baby sis" he adds sarcastically

This time he didn't force me back up to stand right away and this time, I keep my mouth shut. I lay there my face merely an inch from the cold ceramic wincing and holding the right side of my face, the side that he backhanded me on unmercifully twice. I already feel my eye swelling shut. I have never ever been afraid of my brother, but a person can change a lot in three years. Maybe losing our parents and all of this power has gone to his head. I just never thought he would hurt me. The thought literally had never crossed my mind, that I needed to fear my step-brother.

"Go to your room and stay there until I say otherwise. Katherine! And DO NOT make me repeat myself again. GO NOW!" The last word was roared and I realized I needed to get up and move, God only knows

I

what would happen if I stayed laying on the floor disobeying him. But I'm temporarily paralyzed out of fear. Of course, he won't wait for me to get my bearings straight and decides to help me up by my hair. He grabs a handful of hair from the back of my head and yanks, hard. The pain is excruciating and I force myself to stand up. I'm extremely shaky and still a bit disoriented. I'm also shaking out of fear, fear of Tommy. I try to take a step towards the stairs but he holds me in place by my hair and forces me to look at him. My right eye is almost totally swollen at this point but I dare to look up at him for a mere second, and he gives me "the look". The look that he is beyond pissed and don't even think about trying anything. At this point, I'm so terrified, I wouldn't dare. I'm literally shaking as he grips my hair and tears start flowing down my face on their own accord. He let's go and I start walking up the stairs, gripping the railing

so tight my knuckles are white.
I jump as he slams the door to Daddy's office, now it's his office shut. I can barely see as the hot tears are flowing so fast now that they are blurring my vision. Not only am I crying from the pain and of embarrassment at just what transpired, but

most of all because I'm crying from knowing I'm not welcome in my own home anymore. I need to get out. I close my bedroom door behind me and go to the mirror in my bathroom and look at the damage. My face is swollen, black and blue. And red dots of blood drop into the perfectly clean, white sink from my lip Tommy split open. I grab a washcloth off the counter and wet it with cold water and holding it to the painful split on my lip. I sink to the bathroom floor and I just let myself cry and cry.

I must have fallen asleep as I sit up, still on the bathroom floor. I shiver from laying on the cold tile for God knows how long. The house is quiet, my head throbs horrendously and my stomach churns from not having anything to eat since this morning's breakfast from right before I left boarding school. But I don't want to eat either. I get nausea just thinking about food right now. I do want my bag that I think is still downstairs most importantly I want my cell phone that's in my bag. I tiptoe to my door and slowly start to pull it open. I hear it creek and wait with baited breath but nothing seems to stir so I finish pulling it open and as quietly as possible pad down the hall and down the stairs. I see my bag still sitting by the front door. I hurry up and grab it and pad quickly and quietly back into my room. I set my bag down on my bed and pull out my phone. The only person that I can think of that might be able to help me is Teressa my best friend. She's still at school but she has an older brother Drew that has an apartment nearby as I've meet him a couple times when he visited our school and he seemed nice. Of course, I could tell he had a thing for me, so I can use that to my advantage right now. I text because its I don't want to risk being heard talking and I make sure the volume on my phone is all the way down before i text Teresa a little about my predicament. I just told her the basics. That my brother snapped and I needed to get out of here while I try to figure out what to do next. I ask if her brother still lived over here and if he could meet me a couple blocks down at a bus station not far from my house. It's only about a half of a block from the very back of our fenced in yard. I also told her that I thought it was better if she didn't mention to Drew who my brother is. I don't want to take the chance of him not helping me because of who my family is. That seems to happen a lot. People scared by the very name, Sicardo.

It seemed like I waited hours when it was actually just a few minutes for the screen on my cell to light up announcing silently a new text alert. I read the text and Drew is a go. Now I need to figure out how in the hell to get out of here without being seen or heard. Between the guards, the cameras and the barbed-wire fencing that surrounded the entire property, it wasn't going to be easy.

Chapter 4

The best way I can think of is how I used to, before my parents died. I don't think I've ever told Tommy about how I used to sneak out or how. From the time I was old enough to start pulling that kind of shit, like sneaking out, he was already Daddy's right-hand man which meant I couldn't trust him with my secret of sneaking out to meet my friends. I actually had only done it a few times before my parents died and I was shipped off to boarding school but hopefully it still works. I would open my window and climb down off the second story roof using the drain pipe and then run as fast as I could to the very back part of the fence where it lines the vast woods. I'll just have to remember to take a jacket with me to throw over the barbed wire. But I'm desperate. I have to try.

I

Of course, after all this time my window is stuck as I try to push it open. I have to push hard and finally it starts to give but the window also squeaks as it opens. Shit...shit.... it squeaks as it slowly goes up, i wait every few seconds to listen for noise and then I push it up a little further until it's open enough for me to squeeze through. I quickly walk to my walk-in closet and grab an old jacket and throw it on. I take a moment and listen to the house but hear nothing. I grab my cell and tuck it in my back pocket of my jean's. I crawl out the window and onto the roof. Usually I would close the window to hide my escape route so that I could use it again the next time but I can't take the chance on the squeaking from the window waking up the house. I still don't know who or if anyone else sleeps here besides my brother, but there were always two-night guards. One stays at the gate, the other walks the grounds.

Luckily my bedroom faces the backyard and away from the entrance gate. I don't see the second guard or any light from a flashlight so I make my move. I creep across the roof and over to the drainpipe. It's been a few years and I've of course gained some weight as I grew so I hope the drainpipe still holds me. I silently say a prayer and grab onto the drainpipe. I throw one leg over and curl it around the drainpipe, then the other leg. I start to slide down and it's making too much noise. Its older now and the bolts that connect it to the side of the house are rusted. I'm going to get caught for sure if I keep using the drainpipe.

I don't see any other choice but to drop the last half, so before I could change my mind, I let go and fall to the ground. Owwww, I hurt my ankle on landing, and I have to bite my bottom lip so I don't yell out. The kitchen light turns on. Fuck the pain in my ankle, I've got to go now. I don't even want to think how much trouble I'll be in if I'm caught right now. I half run half hobble for what seems like forever but it couldn't have been more than a few minutes to the fence at the far back and i quickly take off my jacket and throw it over the barbed wire at the top of the fence. My ankle burns as I climb the fence, not caring how much noise it makes as I climb. I'm almost there, almost. Just as I throw my other leg over the fence, I see the back-patio lights turn on. Shit! Shit! I let go and drop on the other side down hurting my ankle even more but I have to go. I have to go NOW! The bus stop is only half a block away from here so i try to run as much as I can but mostly just limping. As soon as the bus stop comes into view, I see Drew's car waiting. I stumble over to it and he starts to get out and I yell at him to stay in. It's a good thing I did because as soon as I close the door, I see my brothers SUV turning the corner slowly. I slouch down in my seat, I'm almost on the floor and I yell at Drew to "Drive!"

"Sorry, I said. Thank you so much for getting me, I have nowhere else to go." I added embarrassed at our awkward reunion. "No problem at all Katie." Drew said. I'm sorry your brother is being an asshole. He really did a

I

number on your face didn't he? If you want you can call the police when we get to my place. I can't stand men that hit women. I don't want you to worry, if he does show up at my place, I'll take care of him and give him a taste of his own medicine."

I stay quiet and let Drew say these things. I am

honored and moved that despite barely knowing me, he would stand up for my honor and for what's right. But he doesn't know who my brother is and I don't want him to.

"We will get you cleaned up and get ice put on your face as soon as we get to my place" Drew continues "I noticed that

you were limping, what happened there?"
"I hurt my ankle while getting out of the house. Tommy is actually my step-brother and well thank you. Thank you, for everything" I said quietly
It was a quick, quiet ride but I couldn't get there fast enough knowing that my brother and his goons were out canvassing the

neighborhood looking for me. I'm sure I was in the biggest trouble ever so I couldn't get caught. I didn't want to find out what Tommy would do to me if he found me.

It was actually a nice, no a wonderful night. The first night that I truly had felt free in so long. Boarding school is a lot like kids jail unless you're on break. You are to be in a certain place at a certain time whether it was a class, your dorm room, the cafeteria, study hall and so on. And that obviously wasn't the easiest transition back home. Drew was so kind. He drew me a nice hot bath and played out a clean pair of his boxer shorts and a T-shirt for me since I didn't pack anything and gave me time and privacy to enjoy a nice, long hot bath. While I was in the tub, he cooked me a late-night meal. A delicious chicken pasta with a cream sauce and he gave me ice for my face and my ankle. We watched TV and ended up snuggling and

we continued cuddling
until we fell asleep. It was
an absolutely great night.
I never wanted it to end.
Drew is really caring and
sensitive and he hates
guys who mistreat
women. If I'm not careful,
I could really see myself
falling for this man. As
soon as we woke up, he
made me fresh blueberry
pancakes and after we

finished eating, we started to kiss. We were slowly leading into sex, we were in the midst of taking off each other's clothes, I started un-buckling Drew's belt, feeling his well-endowed dick engorge as I teasingly took my time undoing the buckle and slowly pulling his belt out of the loops. He had started playing with my breasts and undoing my bra.

Suddenly, there was extremely loud non-stop pounding at the front door. I gulped. I already knew who it was.
"I'm so so sorry Drew, I don't want to create problems for you." I said
"I'll take care of your

brother" he started as we both started putting the little back on that we had started to take off.

"No, no, you don't know who my brother is and I'm sorry. That's my fault. I should have said something. No one can do anything. I got to go Drew but thank you for everything. "

"I'll call the police Katie;

you don't have to go back. "
"That will do nothing but get me more in trouble. Just please stay in here. Please" I begged
Pounding
"Katie, I swear to God, I will fucking kick this door down!" Tommy yelled
" Shut the fuck up and go the fuck away!" Drew yelled back

"NO" I screamed but it was too late

"Motherfucker" my brother said and bashed in the door

My brother comes stomping in, along with two of his guys. Drew is trying to gently push me behind him and is ready to protect me. I refuse to get behind Drew instead I put myself in front of him shielding him from my brother.

"Tommy! Please! " I beg and cry all at once My brother shoves me hard out of the way and I land on the floor with a thud. Tommy raises his closed fist in the air and grabs Drew by the collar of his shirt and punches Drew in the face so hard that blood flow out of his

mouth. Tommy raises his fist again but I grab my brothers' leg with my hands and I start to beg through my tears.
"It's my fault, I'm sorry Tommy. Please don't... he doesn't even know who you or I am! Please Tommy, I'm coming home. Be mad at me, not him" I continually beg and plead and cry.

My brother stops and
looks down at me as I'm
still gripping his leg while
still laying on the ground.
I'm crying hysterically and
I just keep saying
please...please
"He doesn't know who I
am huh?" Tommy
sarcastically asks
I very slowly stand up
purposely in from of
Drew again, making

Tommy look at me.
I look at Tommy while i say the next words. Its breaking my heart knowing I'll most likely never speak to Drew again. I should have told him who Tommy was...who I was. I caused all of this

"Drew I'm really sorry, i should have told you and I should have never got you involved. My full name is Katherine...Katherine Sicardo. This is my step-brother Tommy Sicardo." tears stream down my cheeks but I want Tommy to know I'm not lying. Tommy's goons stand at the door awaiting their boss's next orders.

"Tommy please, let's go. Me and him barely know

each other.
"The mafia Sicardo
family?" Drew asks
quietly, incredulously
I can't bear to answer this
time. My eyes fall from
Tommy's to the floor
"Barely know each other
huh?" Tommy says as he
flicks my arm and gives
me a once over.
I'm looking disheveled as
me and Drew were about

I

to have sex and I know Tommy sees right through me. I'm in a thin tank top, one of my bra straps hanging down lose on my arm, my hair is a mess and I'm wearing a pair of Drew's boxer shorts since I spent the night last night but didn't pack a thing at the time just wanting to get out of my house as quickly as possible.

"Tommy, nothing happened. Please. Please, I promise that nothing happened! Can we please go." I plead and beg

Seconds go by and the tension is palpable in the room

"If I EVER see you around my sister again, you're a fucking dead man." Tommy states matter of fact and grips my upper arm tight enough to leave bruises and yanks me after him to the car. He shoves me in the back of the car and I look up as we pull away from Drew's apartment crying knowing I put a innocent sweet man in danger and knowing I'll most likely never see Drew again. Tommy had got in the back seat with me as he had Victor, one of the guys that showed up at Drew's with him, drove. I don't say a word and keep my head down on the short ride home. I feel Tommy's eyes bore into my head the whole time. But I don't dare speak a word or look up at him the entire ride, tears silently streaming down my face. I silently scold myself for fucking around at boarding school because so far, this is much worse. As we pull into the long-gated driveway to our family home, Tommy's cell rings. He answers it and even though the phone is up to his ear, I immediately recognize who's on the other line. Its Uncle

Angelo.

Tommy throws his hand up, motioning Victor to wait on unlocking the car and opening the doors. To my dismay, Tommy gives my Uncle a brief history of all that has transpired over the last twenty-four hours. I hear Uncle Angelo yelling but can't make out exactly what the words are but I

know they are about me.
I do hear my Uncle ask for
the motherfuckers'
address and I chance
looking up at Tommy for
the briefest of seconds
pleading him with my
eyes before looking back
down at the floor.
Tommy said he had that
part covered and he will
let Uncle Angelo know if
he needs anything and

that he will be in touch. Tommy hangs up and looks at me saying, "Angelo said he has a meeting out this way tomorrow and he will probably stop by after." And then he motions for Victor and the others to let us out of the car. I can barely walk. I'm hoping Tommy said that just to try and scare me even more, if that is even possible right now. I quickly exit the car and without making a sound, I head straight to my bedroom as Tommy answers another call. I'm sitting on bed hugging a pillow. I know this isn't over and that I'm in big trouble and I anxiously wait for Tommy to call me back downstairs.

I've been sitting on my bed for some time now but emotionally, I'm spent. My eyes keep closing on their own accord. Maybe Tommy is not going to call me down to punish me. Maybe he realizes how hard he was on me yesterday, how far he pushed me.

As soon as I thought this, I hear people talking

outside my door and within seconds, Tommy opens the door to my bedroom and starts to come in. I keep my head down and keep my mouth shut hoping he will just turn around and leave.

Tommy starts, " Victor will be positioned outside your door and another guard patrolling down

there." He points to the grass below my second story window. He starts pacing the rooms he continues. "Tomorrow, I'm having steel bars installed on your windows to ensure no more escapades. "
"What?" I stammered...I knew better than to open my mouth but this shit is getting out of hand! Bars

on my windows? Like a jail ?!

"Tommy no!" The words leave my mouth before I can stop myself.

Tommy closed the door to my room; I can feel his eyes bearing down on me. I should have kept my mouth shut and let this shit blow over....

"NO?" Tommy starts," you think you actually

have a choice Katherine?
"

I stay silent, I feel as if everything I do or say is wrong
"I'm, s..sorry Tommy". I stammer out. I didn't mean to mess up your life.
"I'm sure you are sorry, now that you that your about to get it" tommy states

I

Chapter 5

I chance a quick glance up at him through my tear-soaked eyelashes.
"Keep your head down! Tommy scolds " stand up and lean over your bed".
I start moving but Something stops me as I

swear, I just heard him undoing his belt... is this how I'm going to lose my virginity? He is sext as sin, but I thought he was pissed, I'm so confused.

"Did I stutter Katherine? He says drawing my name out slowly

"No" I start

"No what?" Tommy questions and I know what he wants. All these men and their egos

"No Tommy" I teased

(Whack) His belt hit my right butt cheek and it hit hard! I cried out

No, what Katherine?! Tommy demanded and all at once I knew this wasn't a game to him

"No sir" I barely get out before another hit with his belt.

I

(Whack)
I Yelp out loudly as the belt hits my upper thighs,
I go to look back confused, hurting physically and emotionally.
"Back in the position!
"Tommy demands
I'm shaking too hard, tears flowing freely as the whips from his belt continue to blow down in

me. After what felt like forever, they stopped. I'm spent as I collapse forward onto my bed.
All of the sudden I feel his hands tenderly rubbing my upper thighs and my very red very sore bottom. Gently. Almost lovingly, I start till feel my wetness starting down there.
"There there" tommy

coos, you took at least one punishment fairly well, surprisingly. He leans forward over me and whispers in my ear, " and stop dressing like a slut Katherine, your almost 18 and then I'll own your body too."

Later that night, I heard the guards open the front door and then heard a

Barbie-like voice ordering Nora, our family cook to make her a risotto pasta for dinner. Nora was like family. She had been around since before my parent's death. Shoot, she was almost like a grandmother to me when I was a young child. She would play with me when my parents were busy and when she wasn't cooking of course and she actually taught me how to make several easy starter dishes. I never heard this voice before but it kind of rubbed me the wrong way someone walking into our home and ordering our staff to do their bidding and on top of that I hear the click clack of high heel pumps scratching along the

Italian wood floors that are in our kitchen. After a few minutes of the loud Barbie voice and really loud obnoxious and unprovoked laughter, I finally decided go downstairs and see what all this fuss was about. I walk down the stairs through the great room and into the kitchen and there sits a living, breathing, talking fricking Barbie doll! The only exception is that she has shoulder length curly blond hair, but the rest of the resemblance is uncanny! She's sitting on one of the stools at the breakfast bar that faces the kitchen inward as she pokes her perfectly manicured nails through a bowl of strawberries touching at least two to three strawberries before she finds an acceptable one to eat. I'll have to rewash the rest of the strawberries later since she touched almost all of them, so I silently make as mental note.

"I'm Tommy's girlfriend, Candice and who might you be? She spoke as she

I

played with the strawberry in her hand.

I just turned around and went back up the stairs. I was stupid to think Tommy wouldn't have a gorgeous blond hair, huge tit girlfriend. She's everything I'm not. I really thought me and Tommy had a moment earlier, but I guess I am a child and it was all in my head.

Chapter 6
Tommy

I couldn't believe Katherine got kicked out of boarding school and right before her 18th Birthday. That's how I kept her safe, but she was to young and naive to realize it. The boarding

school, the Europe and
Africa trips during her
breaks from school. I had
to keep her far away from
my enemies and from
me. She's my Achilles
tendon and my enemies
know it. One look of her
gorgeous lean, toned
body, with legs for miles
while walking down the
steps off of the private
chartered plane and I

knew i would be in trouble. At first, I kept telling myself to act indifferent, don't even let your closest men know that you give a damn. Maybe indifference and just plain being mean might save her. I've lost everyone and everything I have ever given a damn about it loved in this life except Katherine.

I was so pissed at myself fast I had lost my cool and actually hit her! But at the same time, I couldn't let her walk all over me especially in front of my crew! I'm the youngest made man in this region and boy did I have to work at it and constantly prove to my father before he passed back when. But I still have

to prove myself to my
men and my superiors
including my uncle, that I
was more than capable of
handling business. I
cannot show weakness
when called out like that
no matter who the fuck it
is. I don't remember the
last time I felt so
emotional drained and
pissed last night but I was
disappointed that I let it

get that far with Katherine on her first night home. I'm not an overly emotional guy. I didn't even cry when our parents were murdered 3 years ago but when they died, it was the closet I've come to breaking down in a extremely long long time. I was so pissed last night that I just shut myself off in my office

and canceled all meetings
and refused to answer
the never-ending calls on
my phone. I got to
remember she is not the
enemy, nor is she one of
my enemy's wives and
she is definitely not the
run of the muck bimbo's
that I'm used to fucking. I
was completely and
utterly at a loss at how in
the fucking world, I was

going to protect her now that she's home, where all of our family's many enemies live. And at the same time, I have got to rein in that sassy, smart ass, attitude of hers.

In the meantime, I hear my want-to-be girlfriend, Candice downstairs, so I need to get out of here, I'm in no mood for her shit today. I got to get Katherine out of the house and hopefully avoid that bimbo Candice bitch all together.

Chapter 7
Katherine

"Katherine, come down stairs! " I heard Tommy commanding over my blow-dryer.

"One minute", I had barely got that out when Tommy yelled back in a roaring voice

"I said get the Fuck down here now!

Oh geez, he's in a mood, I thought to myself as a ran down the stairs.

"Yea, what's up Tommy?
"

" we are going for a ride"

he said nonchalantly
"My friend Teressa is
picking me up in a little
bit Tommy. I can't go
now." But he cut me off
"Did I ask you what the
fuck you wanted
Katherine? " Tommy said
loudly, arrogantly.
Why when he calls me by
my full name, like I'm a
small child getting caught
in the cookie jar, does it

I

make me do wet? So, turned on? I noticed he was still looking at me, and he was starting to turn red, losing his patience with me because I didn't answer quick enough.

"Um, no....no sir." I said looking down because I felt my face turning crimson from the rapid blushing occurring due to dirty thoughts.

Tomorrow, I will be 18! I can't believe it! I took out my phone to text my friend Teressa and Tommy swiped it out of my hand and put it in his pocket.

"Hey," I started

"When you're with me, I get one hundred percent of your attention. Do you hear me Katherine?" Tommy asked with a stern voice

"Hey baby!" Candice walked up cooing

"Not now Candice, I'm busy." Tommy said already bored with this bimbo. He knew who he wanted and it wasn't Candice.

I reached back for my phone and surprisingly Tommy let me take it and he tried to stop me as I walked out the door but Candice grabbed his arm and I took the opportunity to bolt as tears pricked at my eyes. Since he never let me text Teresa that I wasn't able to come, she thank God was pulling up in our driveway as I walked out the door. Why am I so damn upset about him having a girlfriend? Look at him! Of course, he has a girlfriend! I scolded myself, he's well, he's gorgeous! And I shouldn't be surprised that I am nothing to him. Whatever, Drew is working at a club tonight and is going to get me and Teresa in. I'm about to cry when I get in her car. I see Tommy start walking towards us and I tell Teressa to hurry and drive. I then rolled down my window and purposely dropped my phone onto the drive as we drove away.

I knew Tommy saw that I had purposely threw my phone out the window when had it shattered. I wasn't stupid, I know that that's how he tracked me a Drew's the last time and I'm sick of his games. I'm sick of the mix signals, I thought the other night that we shared something but I guess it was just a plain ole ass whooping after all. Me and Teresa drove to Drew's house and picked him up. It was basically a quiet ride. She knew that I was in no mood to talk. Drew was working as a DJ at a bar that night and had worked there before so he knew he could get us in. We went in with him at the beginning of his shift so he could see sneak us in through the back door since we were obviously under age. But at midnight I would be 18! And free! Free from Tommy, free from this life or at least what my life had become. I make a mental note to start searching apartments first thing in the morning as I know I have to get away. The ride was also pretty quiet on the way to the bar. It was extremely awkward fir me because of the position I put Drew in and on top of it in his own home. I brought trouble to Drew's house and I felt horrible and ashamed. Especially that I wasn't upfront with him about who I really was or who my stepbrother was. He told me he forgave me and that it wasn't a big deal and tried to act like it wasn't but I'll never forget the look on Drew's face when my stepbrother stood towering over him, muscles clenched, jaw tight and ready or more like counting on a fight and then to top it off, I had to tell him that I was a Sicardo and part of the Sicardo mob family. One might think it would be cool to throw the name around and it I admit, it had helped me a time or two in the past but honestly, that name Sicardo alone caused way more trouble for me than it was worth.

As soon as we arrived at Gillian's bar and night club, I ran into the bathroom and just wept. I wept because I started to have feelings for Tommy and I felt like an idiot because just look at him! His glistening tattooed arms with his huge biceps, six pack abs, he was every women's dream. He was hot and sexy as sin! Of course, he had a girlfriend! I was stupid to even think that he would even want somebody like me. Teresa found me in the bathroom crying and leave to her, my best friend knew what I needed and brought me couple shots to start the night. I downed the 1st one not even asking what it was but as soon as it got through my lips, I knew it was vodka. I grabbed the second and downed it and asked her to get me some more while I'll changed into the clothes that she brought me. I changed into a tight black mini skirt along with black platform high heels and a really tight mid-drift shiny rhinestone strapless top. I grabbed Teresa's makeup from her bag and went to work. I did a full face with red lipstick. I took out her curling iron and put just a few curls in my down to my ass dark brown hair. Teresa returned with two more shots in tow and I took both and downed them. She gave me a look; I took as that one of them was supposed to be for her.

"Sorry", I said, "I'm thirsty" and I started to giggle as the Vodka from the two previous shots started kicking in.

"You need to slow down! You're going to get sick or pass out and miss your birthday celebration! She lightly scolded and then started giggling herself. I took one last look in the mirror in the bathroom and I must admit I looked damn good! It's a rare occasion that I do my full makeup and to top it off dress this way, but you only turn 18 once! We can hear the music starting to flow in the bathroom and could feel the walls do the slightest shake at the beat of the bass so I checked my watch and was almost ten P.M. already! I walked over to the bar and sat down ready for

I

another drink and I wasn't quite yet ready to dance just yet. After another shot, I was feeling pretty good when a decent looking guy came up to me and introduced himself as Blake and asked me if he could dance with me. Teresa smiled and nodded her head to go so I agreed plus I came to have fun on my birthday anyway. Me and Blake headed through the thickening crowd to the dance floor and started dancing to the beats of the song. There are so many people here now I can't even see where Drew or Teresa are. Pretty soon Blake's friend brought us another couple shots. I'm so drunk at this point that I don't even know what it was but it didn't taste very good. I was getting pretty drunk and I needed to pee from all the alcohol but Blake and his burly friend were not Ready to let me leave. Blake was in front and his friend was in back and they both started grinding their hard dicks all over my body. I tried to dart through the side but Blake grabbed my hands and his friend grabbed my ass and they held me in place while they continued grinding. I was trying to pull and tug and get away when I felt him before I saw him. Tommy had found me. Before I knew it all chaos had ensued. Tommy grabbed Blake and knocked him out with the 1st punch he then turned around and grabbed Blake's friend by the throat and started strangling him. I really thought he was going to kill him but he let go at the last minute and when the man fell to the ground Tommy started kicking the shit out of him. He then grabbed me by the arm hard and yanked pulling me after him. I was trying to stop him but I was too drunk and in mega high heels so I started to fall so Tommy just picked me up as if I was nothing and threw me over his shoulder and spanked my ass hard. As soon as we were outside and could hear each other I started screaming. Tommy just smacked my ass even harder. By now Theresa and Drew had started coming out but luckily Tommy DC didn't see Drew and proceeded to throw me from his shoulder into the back of his SUV and then followed in the back telling his driver to "DRIVE NOW!"

I was crying and
screaming at Tommy that
he's ruining my life and
just to leave me alone
and go back to his Barbie-
doll girlfriend. Tommy
answered by asking "Do
you know what time it
is?"
I just started yelling at
him more about the
mixed signals and how he
was ruining my birthday.

Tommy demanded a second time, "What time is it Katherine?"

"Twelve o'six A.M. what does that matter Tommy?" I cried out as we pulled into the driveway

"It matters because you're eighteen years old now and so now I own you fully." Tommy said with a glint in his eye. He wasn't making any sense.

"Go up to your room Katherine and await your punishment."

"Great, so you really are going to ruin my birthday." I said as I sulked up the stairs with Tommy right on my tail.

"Take off your clothes Katherine, all of them. You are not allowed to look like a slut out in public. You can only dress like that for me." Tommy stated as he started undoing his belt.

I didn't argue. I was spent from crying and screaming and I was just done with the whole day. I might as well get this ass whooping over so I can go to bed. I turn around and Tommy stood completely naked, his magnificent cock engorged and full and begging to be sucked dry. I couldn't take my eyes off of it. I knelt down in front of him, and looked up. Tommy nodded in approval as he started toying with my hair. So, I didn't give him the chance to change his mind, I took the huge, thick cock in my hand and then followed with my mouth. It was too big to get all of it in my mouth but I took and took until I was practically checking on it. I kept thinking I must be dreaming but Tommy took my head in his hands and stopped my movement. With his cock still down my throat, he commanded me to look up at him. I peeked up through my thick eyelashes. Tommy started, " She was never my girlfriend. I never really had one because the girl I've loved for a very long time is you Katherine. When I'll say i own you, its mind, body and soul and I hope you feel the same way. Don't get me wrong, if you EVER pull the shit you pulled tonight again, I

WILL whoop your ass.
Maybe I was too hard on
you but I never trusted
anyone after what
happened to your mother
and my father to know
how much you mean to
me. I'm in love with you."
He released me and
through tears, happy
tears this time
responded, "I love you

too Tommy."

(FIND OUT WHAT
HAPPENS WHEN
KATHERINE IS KIDNAPPED
BY A RIVAL FAMILY IN
BOOK 2)